To all those who have begun to learn English:
may this book help you on your journey.
To all the greyhounds in the world: may there
always be grass for you to run on and tasty
snacks for you to enjoy.

www.mascotbooks.com

This is Clare

For more information, please contact:
Mascot Books
620 Herndon Parkway #320
Herndon, VA 20170
info@mascotbooks.com

Library of Congress Control Number: 2019919114

CPSIA Code: PRT0721A
ISBN-13: Insert # 978-1-64307-360-6

Printed in the United States

This Is CLARE

Lindy Nelson

Illustrated by
Ingrid Lefebvre

This is **Clare.**

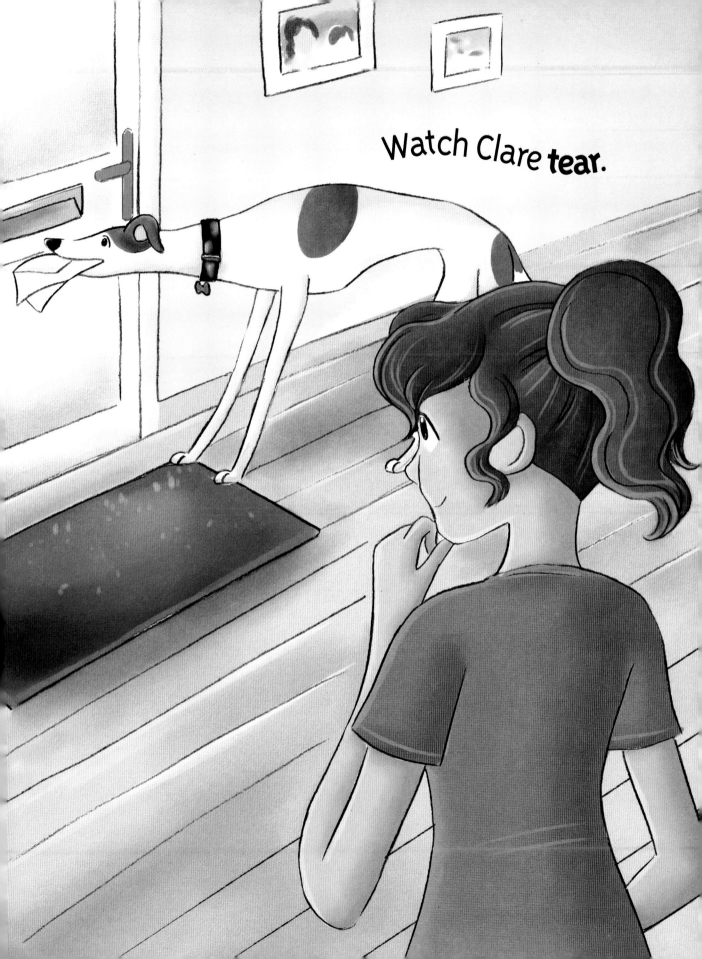

Watch Clare **tear.**

Watch Clare **tear** with **flair**.

This is **Clare.**

Watch Clare **stare.**

Watch Clare **stare** with **despair**.

This *is* Clare.

Watch Clare **scare.**

Watch Clare **scare** in the **square**.

This is **Clare**.

Watch Clare **glare**.

Watch Clare **glare** at the **hare.**

This is Clare.

Watch Clare say a **prayer** with the **mare**.

This is **Clare**.

Watch Clare **dare**.

Watch Clare **dare** at the **fair.**

Watch Clare find a **pair**.

Watch Clare find a **pair** to **spare**.

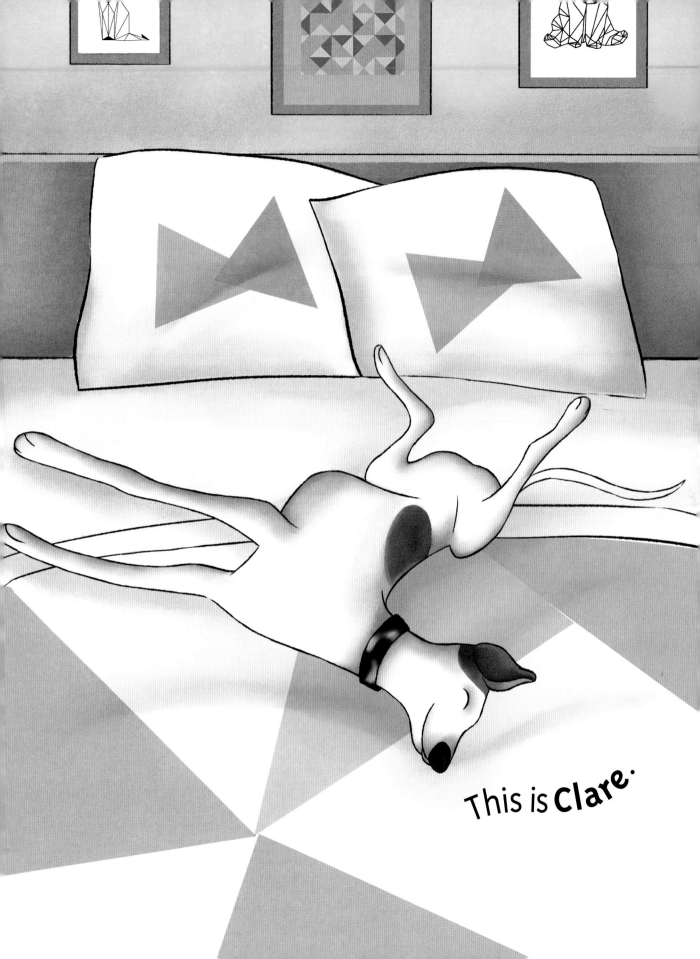

This is **Clare.**

Watch Clare **share**.

Watch
Clare
share
with
care.

About the Author

Lindy is an American who has spent most of her adult life teaching English in China after graduating from University of Wisconsin, Milwaukee. She enjoys arts and crafts, funny memes, eating candy, and of course, spending time with her greyhound, Clarence.

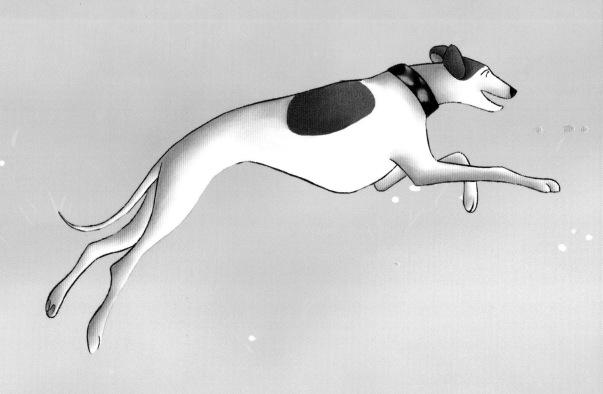